FRIDAY MY RADIO FLYER FLEW

ZACHARY PULLEN

Simon & Schuster Books for Young Readers

New York   London   Toronto   Sydney

. . . and my dad's old
Radio Flyer surfaced.

That Sunday we went for a stroll.

Then on Monday morning

I got motivated.

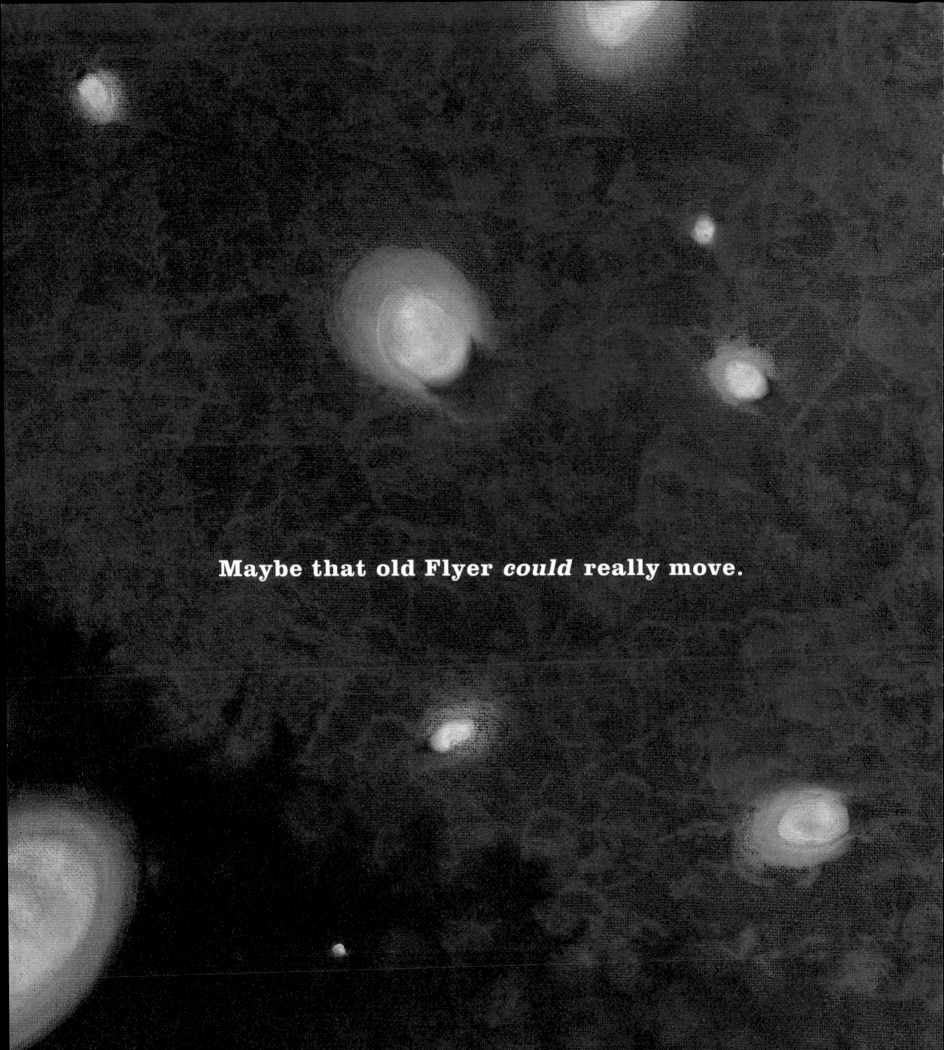

Maybe that old Flyer *could* really move.

So all day Tuesday . . .

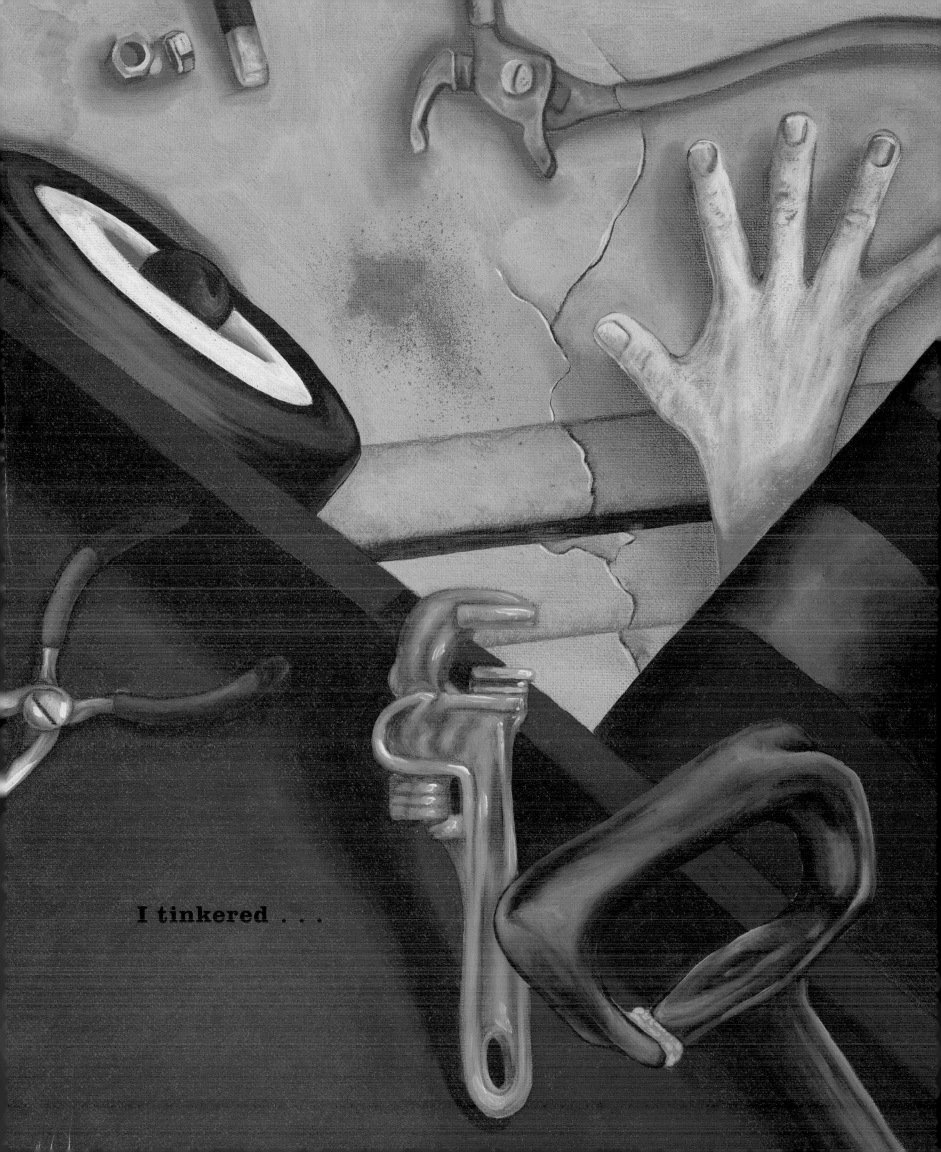

I tinkered . . .

But Wednesday was wet.

We had to wait.

On Thursday I tried to take off . . . .

Finally on Friday . . .

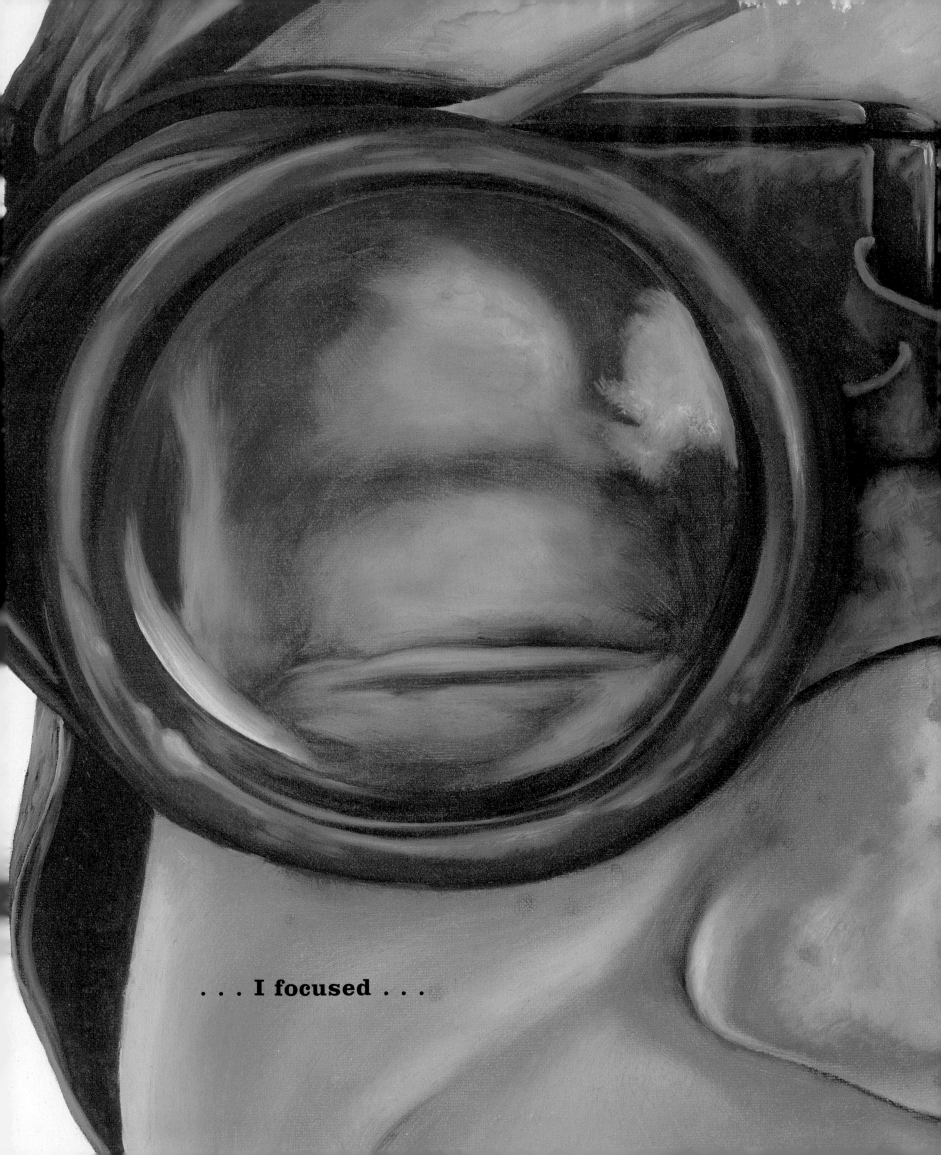

. . . I focused . . .

. . . and my Radio Flyer . . .

. . . flew . . .

. . . and flew . . .

RADIO

. . . and flew!

To Renate,

for giving me the best little Radio Flyer pilot

a dad could ever hope for

Special thanks to Bridger and Morgan.

SIMON & SCHUSTER BOOKS FOR YOUNG READERS
An imprint of Simon & Schuster Children's Publishing Division
1230 Avenue of the Americas, New York, New York 10020
Copyright © 2008 by Zachary Pullen
All rights reserved, including the right of reproduction
in whole or in part in any form.
SIMON & SCHUSTER BOOKS FOR YOUNG READERS
is a trademark of Simon & Schuster, Inc.
RADIO FLYER is a registered trademark of
Radio Flyer Inc. and is used with permission.
Book design by Tom Daly
The text for this book is set in Clarendon BT.
The illustrations for this book are rendered in
M. Graham oil paints and walnut medium.
Manufactured in China
6 7 8 9 10
CIP data for this book is available
from the Library of Congress.
ISBN-13: 978-1-4169-3983-2
ISBN-10: 1-4169-3983-0
1113 SCP